THE DOCTOR'S MAGIC HANDS

DOCTOR ROMANCE NOVEL

MICHELLE LOVE

CONTENTS

Made in "The United States" by:

Michelle Love

© Copyright 2021

ISBN: 978-1-64808-003-6

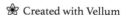 Created with Vellum

BLURBS

Blurb (Male viewpoint)

Throughout his school years, when other boys were out discovering the mysteries of the opposite sex, Dr. Mark Cartwright was focused on graduating medical school and setting up his successful cardiac surgery practice. Now nearly thirty, comfortably well off, the highly eligible bachelor doctor has little time for or interest in women. That changes when he meets successful criminal attorney, Sandra Marshall, heir to steel magnate Richard Marshall's billion-dollar company. She just gets Mark, in spite of his total lack of social graces. But will that continue, or will she eventually give up on his overall social clumsiness and workaholic tendencies?

BLURB (FEMALE VIEWPOINT)

SHE ADMITS IT. Sandra Marshall, successful criminal attorney, the woman with her nose to the grindstone ever since law school, is attracted to brilliant, young cardiac surgeon, Mark

Cartwright. Since her last relationship went down in flames, she's buried herself even more than ever in her work. But Mark Cartwright not only saves her father's life; he's reopened her eyes to the world. But can the two workaholics find a way to balance love and constant work?

CHAPTER ONE

The sun had not yet begun to peek through the bare maple trees on Borthwick Avenue when twenty-seven-year-old Dr. Mark Cartwright stepped out of his Chevy Cavalier and started toward the massive buildings of Coastal Cardio-thoracic and Vascular Surgery.

HALF THE WORLD *never sees the best part of the day,* Mark thought as he trudged through the crunchy snow that covered the parking lot. As he walked, he glanced up at the facility, a center of excellence for its multi-disciplinary surgeons and dedication to the highest standards of treatment since 1998, and thought about early morning surgical rounds.

MARK SHIVERED in New Hampshire's frigid December air, stuffed his hands deeper into the pockets of his heavy down coat, and mulled over the weeks to come. His usual Christmas routine involved work. He took double shifts to give his colleagues with children more time at home. However, very recently, Mark's

father, always big, blustery, and larger than life, had been diagnosed with advanced pancreatic cancer. By the time Hugh was
diagnosed, it had spread. As a result, Mark's typical Christmas
plans had been upended. Now, he and his sister Cindy would be
flying to Florida, she from Michigan and he from North
Carolina, to spend what could potentially be their last
Christmas as a family.

SNOW STUNG Mark's face as he entered the sliding glass doors of
the emergency department. It covered his curly blonde hair and
melted down the back of his neck. He let himself believe the
snow was also responsible for the sheen of tears briefly in his
green eyes.

"HI, STRANGER," Carrie LeBeau called teasingly from the nurses'
station where Mark had seen her less than five hours ago when
he'd been called in for a cardiac emergency. He'd debated even
going home, but the veteran nurse, a grandmotherly figure at
the hospital and especially to Mark, had shooed him out for at
least a few hours of rest.

"Hey, Care," he called back, nodding at various residents as
he walked by them, noticing their various states of shock, so
common for newbies. "Did the coffee machine ever get
repaired?"

IN RESPONSE, she raised a to-go cup from the local diner. "No, but
I've got you covered. You owe me, kid."

. . .

"I OWE YOU SO MUCH, you'll be a millionaire by the time I pay up," he replied with a tired smile, stepping into the locker room.

WITH A SIGH, Mark shed his winter layers and pulled on green scrubs. Thankfully, because the bulk of its patients were cardiac care cases whose body temperatures tended to be low, the hospital was kept relatively warm, unlike the place he'd done his own residency. That had been like a perpetual igloo.

WALKING BACK into the familiar hallways, Mark joined Carrie at her station. She didn't look up from the chart she was perusing, but nodded at the coffee she had waiting for him.

"I LOVE YOU," he sighed, taking a long sip. He didn't drink coffee a specific way, so she liked to tease him by mixing it up. This time it was apparently black with minimal sugar, which suited him fine.

"I'M TAKEN, boy. You need to get yourself a girl your own age," she said wryly, scrawling a note on the chart. "The OR crew's signed in and in surgery doing prep for the first one of the day."

STILL NOT LOOKING UP, Carrie held her hand out and Mark placed his car keys in them. Photographic memory though he had, it was reserved for everything except everyday details, apparently. He could recite a textbook or surgical procedure verbatim. But ask him where his car or car keys were and he was a lost cause.

.   .   .

CARRIE HAD LONG AGO STEPPED in to help out since time spent searching for misplaced keys or paperwork was valuable time he might instead have put to good use saving lives. Or she could've been helping out because it saved her her own time not having to call cabs for Mark.

"DID you ever call that girl back?" This time Carrie lifted her head and pinned Mark with her warm gray gaze.

HE WINCED AND SHE SIGHED. "Kid, you've got to get yourself laid. You might've stood a chance with her, but Jessica won't give you the time of day now."

"I FORGOT," he muttered sheepishly. "I meant to ..."

"NO. You didn't. I don't know why I bother suggesting possibilities," Carrie said dryly. "Go save a life. You're great at that, at least."

"SORRY," he apologized, as he started toward the OR. Except he wasn't. Not really.

SOCIAL RELATIONSHIPS HAD ALWAYS BEEN a puzzle to Mark. Since childhood, Mark had always had trouble making friends. He missed social clues and was often brutally honest, alienating others unintentionally. His sister had tried to help him but he just didn't get it then, and he still didn't get it now. He might be a star surgeon, a medical prodigy who had graduated medical school when most were barely graduating college, but people ... people were a mystery. Especially women.

As he scrubbed for surgery, a fellow surgeon, Jim Owens walked in and joined him at the sink. Owens was the antithesis of Mark, friendly and popular with both sexes.

"Talk me through who's on the table today," Mark requested. He already knew every pertinent surgical detail, but Owens would know other stuff, things that would help humanize the patient. Mark knew that was important, even if he wasn't always entirely clear on why.

"Good morning to you too, Mark," Owens reminded him, ever patient, before starting in as they both scrubbed carefully. "Richard Marshall's our guy today. You know his company, right?"

"No."

"Dude." Owens shook his head. "He's the billionaire who donates millions to this hospital. *Maybe* learn the names of the people who sign your paycheck?" He held up a hand, before Mark could respond in confusion. "No, he doesn't literally sign it, but he gives a lot of the cash that helps make it possible. He's

62, on his third wife, and likes top-of-the-line things. Cars. Houses. Medical care. Food. The food is what landed him here today."

THAT MUCH MARK UNDERSTOOD. Mr. Marshall was significantly overweight and his heart was in bad shape, to the extent that he needed bypass surgery and a replacement valve. Normally this required two separate surgeries. But Mark and his team had perfected a procedure whereby they could do both operations at the same time, thus avoiding undue stress on his patient's compromised heart.

"WE'VE GOT his company's CEO, Willis Gerrard observing today," Owens went on.

"WHY?" Mark asked in surprise, though it was no concern to him who watched or didn't. He operated the same way, regardless.

"BECAUSE MR. MARSHALL is important to the company. If he croaks, life gets difficult for everyone there," Owens explained. "Don't ask how. It just will. Oh, and he likes The Ramones, so they'll be playing while we operate. I know you don't usually do music, but he specifically requested background music."

"BUT HE WON'T HEAR," Mark protested. "True, there's evidence of some consciousness while under anesthesia, but—"

. . .

"HE PAYS THE HOSPITAL BILLS," Owens repeated, backing into the OR with his hands held up and waiting for Mark to follow. "So we play whatever he wants."

DISCONCERTED, but still not concerned—he tuned almost everything out as he worked, so music would be no impediment to his performance—Mark joined Jim in the OR and waited as a nurse helped them both with gloves. The unfamiliar music was indeed playing in the background and Mark ignored it and focused instead on his team.

HIS HEAD SURGICAL NURSE, Honey Braswell, was checking trays and instructing the rest of the nursing staff. Leon Garrit, his anesthesiologist, was monitoring his patient's vitals. He gave Mark a thumbs-up sign to indicate his patient was ready.

MARK GLANCED over at the window. As Jim had said he would be, Willis Gerrard stared down into the operating theater, his brows furrowed and his jaw set.

"HE LOOKS WORRIED," Nellie Gary, Mark's intern, commented. "Because his boss is on the table."

"I GOT THAT," Mark replied with a low chuckle. His team had a tendency to think he needed babysitting on even the most blatant of social cues. He liked to remind them that he was oblivious, not blind, but they didn't usually agree that there was a difference.

. . .

"GERRARD'S afraid of losing his golden goose," Nellie added.

"THEN, we'd better make sure he doesn't," Mark said simply. "His family might also appreciate it."

NELLIE GAVE him a surprised look and he stifled a sigh. He really wasn't the emotionless robot he was reputed to be; he just wasn't great at showing affection in the same way other people did, apparently. If he liked someone, he was blunt about it to a point that seemingly made others uncomfortable. And if he didn't like someone, well, he either avoided them or was just as blunt, and none of those reactions ever went over particularly well.

"OKAY, TEAM," said Owens. "Let's make Willis proud of us," he said, opening the intercom between the observation deck and the surgery. "You're on candid camera," he chirped.

SURGERY BEGAN as it always did. The team performed like a well-rehearsed ballet troupe. Each had his own space and tasks. Each knew instinctively what others would do before them and how others would grab the baton and carry on after they'd completed their jobs.

THE TEAM CONVERSED CASUALLY, with familiarity born of many surgeries worked together. They worked their way through a variety of topics as surgery progressed, until several hours in, the conversation worked its way back around to Mr. Marshall, or at least Mr. Marshall's immediate family.

"Did you see his daughter?" Phil asked. "She's a hotshot criminal lawyer," he added. "She could take my case any day. What do you think, Mark?"

Mark thought back to the moment a few days earlier when he'd caught a glimpse of Mr. Marshall's daughter, right after speaking with his wife. Truthfully, she was beautiful. So beautiful that he'd actually noticed, which rarely happened. "I heard she's a long distance runner."

"That's what you noticed about her?" Phil asked in disbelief. "That's all you noticed?"

"What did I miss?" Mark asked, just to tease the man.

"How about she's smokin' hot and she wants your body?"

"I'm sure you imagined that," Mark said, hiding a smirk. "Suction, please."

"Yeah, right," Honey commented, handing over the suction pump. "Like I imagined that Maserati she drives parked outside my house. Her shoes cost more than the mortgage payment I can barely scrimp together."

"That loser ex of yours hasn't come through with back child support?" asked Nell. "Why don't you take him to court?"

"Because I can't afford the legal costs," admitted Honey. "He knows he's got me over a barrel. Let's talk about something else. Are we about ready for the valve replacement, Mark?"

"Just closing on the by-pass," Mark responded. "Get the valve ready."

"Are you still living in that old inn, Mark?" asked Susan. "My mom is going to sell her cabin. Are you interested?"

"Thanks, Susan," replied Mark. "I think I'll just stick with my room at the Stratford Arms."

"Isn't it a little weird not to have a place of your own?" Phil asked.

"Not at all," Mark replied, tying the last stitch in the valve replacement. "I see no

need for a house. I'm never there anyway. This way the staff cleans the room, washes the sheets, provides breakfast. I've got the best of both worlds."

"I guess there's a lot to be said for a staff that's always there to do your bidding. Mrs. Loudon seems to like that you're there. She talks about you as if you're visiting royalty," noted Jim.

Mrs. Loudon was another motherly figure in Mark's life. While he appreciated the older women who seemed to appear in his life at the exact moment he needed their assistance with something or other, Mr. Marshall's daughter had brought to mind something he usually avoided—his single state. He honestly didn't mind it. Or he usually didn't. But one look at Mr. Marshall's daughter's beautiful face—what was her name?—and suddenly his nights weren't as peaceful as they used to be.

"But is being a permanent hotel guest really living?" asked Honey, cutting into Mark's mini-fantasy.

"It suits my needs," Mark shrugged, glad for the interruption. However beautiful Sandra was, he had no place in his life for anything other than work. No point pretending. "You can close now and we'll get Mr. Marshall into recovery."

"Good work, team," said Jim. "Are you going to talk to Mrs. Marshall and her daughter, Mark?" asked Jim. "Or are you going to leave that to Mr. Gerrard?"

"No. I'll do that," Mark said immediately. *His daughter is here? Of course his daughter is here. You just operated on her father. Maybe it's a different daughter?*

But as he closed and washed up after the surgery, his thoughts, always laser focused, kept drifting to the beautiful woman whose name he badly wanted to remember.

CHAPTER TWO

There she was. Mark took his time approaching Mr. Marshall's room, giving himself time both to build confidence—he really didn't do all that well with patients who weren't on the table—and also to appreciate how beautiful the woman standing in the doorway was. There were two women, but only one of them caught his eye.

The older woman was Mr. Marshall's third wife, Vivian, and some might have considered her beautiful, even though her curves were very definitely silicone and her face had had about as much work as Mr. Marshall's chest. Mark's surgeon's eye could see exactly where the incisions had been made and what nips and tucks had been done. The second woman was Sandra —Mark had gotten her name from Carrie—and she was everything her stepmother was not.

Though Sandra was also outfitted in expensive clothes, hers seemed to suit her well, her long blue peacoat molding beautifully to the natural curves that had sparked Mark's interest a few days back. He remembered her eyes and wondered if they'd match the coat.

He got closer and had just a moment to confirm that Sandra's blue eyes, though shadowed with worry, were a perfect match for the coat, before both women started toward him.

"How is he?" Sandra asked immediately, and Mark noticed hints of tears on her cheeks. That wasn't a surprise immediately after a high-risk surgery. What was a surprise was that he noticed. He also, oddly, wanted to offer her a tissue. She looked nervous and tense, hovering in the doorway as though she wasn't sure if she should flee or stick around.

"The operation went well," said Mark. "There were no complications."

"Oh, thank you, Dr. Cartwright." Vivian grabbed his hand and wrung it, her own face overly made up, such that he struggled to read any sincerity on it. "We're so grateful." He was the one who was grateful when she let go of him and blotted invisible tears from her heavily mascara'd eyes with a dramatic flourish of a lace handkerchief.

"Mr. Marshall is in recovery now," Mark went on, looking between the two women and noting what seemed to be an undercurrent of tension between them. "You should be able to see him shortly. He'll be asleep for a few hours. Then we'll transfer him to ICU. If all goes well, he should be going home Thursday. "

"Thank you." Sandra's voice trembled slightly and then, before he knew what was happening, Mark found himself being hugged fiercely by the woman who had been recently haunting his dreams.

"Uh," he stuttered, enthralled by the feel of her warm, soft body pressed tightly against his, while simultaneously praying she didn't feel his instant arousal and find it totally unprofessional.

"No, *thank you*," Sandra repeated, stepping back and leaving

Mark feeling oddly empty. Then she took his hand and pressed it warmly, smiling up at him. "Dad just doesn't take care of himself, but maybe this will be a new beginning—"

"We've kept the good doctor from his rounds too long already, Sandra." Vivian interrupted. "We should go and look in on your father. Aren't you worried at all about him?"

Sandra's incredible eyes flashed, confirming the animosity Mark had initially noticed between the two elegant women who might have been sisters, their ages were so close. If he still wasn't fully certain, Sandra's next words made it crystal clear.

"I'm actually worried about him, yes, Vivian. But feel free to call Bank of America and let them know you'll still be getting your allowance this Sunday."

Fixing Sandra with a murderous glare, Vivian flounced out of the room.

Mark blinked and shuffled awkwardly, at a loss in the best of social situations. Obviously more adept at reading social clues than he was, Sandra turned to Mark and gave him an apologetic smile.

"I'm sorry about that. It drives me crazy that she obviously married Dad for his money. I managed to get him to have her sign a prenup, which at least means she gets nothing if he dies. So she has a vested interest in his health. She really hasn't liked me since."

With that, the tall blonde flashed Mark a dazzling smile and followed Vivian down the hall toward the recovery room. And Mark's eyes followed Sandra, tracing her long legs as they walked away from him and sliding slowly upwards.

"You didn't notice her at all, huh."

Mark jumped and turned to see Phil watching him from a few feet away, a wide grin on the bald man's bearded face. "I—"

"Don't even try it this time, Cartwright," Phil cut in. "I saw.

Better yet, you saw. Ladies and gentlemen, the superstar surgeon has more than just a brain!" Pumping a fist in the air, he walked away, leaving Mark flushed and foolish mid-hallway, thinking about Sandra's voice, her eyes, her lips, legs, and shapely backside.

CHAPTER THREE

"He's coming along fine." Sandra started the water running in the bathtub and reached for a capful of bubbles to add as she and her best friend, Rita, talked. "You know dad. He's badgering the hospital staff to release him and hounding his employees to bring him reports. Vivian is frantic to keep him from overexerting himself."

Through the phone, she could hear Rita smile as she replied. "That prenup was one of the best ideas you've ever had. So. Tell me about this doctor."

"What do you mean?" asked Sandra, playing totally dumb. Dr. Cartwright had been running through her mind nonstop since their two meetings. The man wasn't as tall or built as the men she usually was attracted to, but there was something about his curly hair, bright green eyes, and shy demeanor that had made its mark on her. That and his hands. Wow, the man had beautiful hands. She'd noticed them again today when she'd thanked him.

"Hello?" Rita said in her ear. "Anyone there?"

Dragging herself quickly from her fantasy of hugging the

surgeon again, this time with fewer clothes between them, Sandra quickly said, "Sorry, I'm running the tub and almost dropped the phone. What'd you say?"

"I said, tell me about the doctor."

"Who have you been talking to?" Sandra stalled. "It was Vivian. Wasn't it? Are you going to believe anything that gold digger says?"

"She just said your father's doctor was young and good looking," Rita replied. "I was hoping you'd notice, for a change."

"Well, Vivian never misses a man with looks or money," Sandra sneered. "I on the other hand noted that he was competent and well spoken."

"Come on, Sandra," Rita said in total exasperation. "You're not going to tell me you didn't notice that he was attractive. Don't play that game. You're not blind."

"I noticed," Sandra said grudgingly, peeling off her jeans and tossing them aside. "But I placed no priority on the doctor's appearance. What mattered was that he saved Dad's life."

"Yeah, right. Start talking or I'm hanging up."

As Sandra started to pull off her bra and blouse, Mark moved through her mind again, along with the thought of those hands doing the job for her. "He was hot, all right? Really hot. And weirdly shy for a superstar surgeon. It was... sweet."

"Oh my God, you like him!" Rita cheered. "There is a God! You've gotta call him!"

"Why?" Sandra finished undressing and dipped a toe into the water, swirling the bubbles around.

"Why not?" demanded Rita. "You want to see him again. Don't you?"

"Yes," Sandra confessed. "But I'm not going to push the issue. It's not my style. Vivian has the market cornered on that!"

Rita sighed. "Maybe it's high time you took a page from her book."

"Why would I do that?" asked Sandra.

"You're on my last nerve," Rita warned. "Just call him. Or else." She hung up and Sandra put the phone aside. She grabbed her robe and wandered into the kitchen to pour a glass of wine, thinking things through as she located a fresh bottle, her last one having disappeared a few weeks back when she and Rita had an extremely rare girls' day.

It had been nearly a year since she and Adam had mutually ended things. Though Rita did go overboard with the melodrama, maybe it wouldn't be a bad thing to try stepping back into the dating game.

Should I call him? Will he think I'm totally out of line, since Dad is his patient?

Sandra sighed. Why did relationships have to be so complicated? Compared to dating, law was a walk on the beach. You could always refer to the law books or look at precedent-setting cases. Not so with relationships.

Before they'd gone their separate ways, Adam had informed Sandra that she had always been better in the courtroom than the bedroom. Much as that had hurt, it probably was true.

"Oh well," she said aloud, abruptly coming to a decision as Mark's handsome face came to mind again. That was the way Sandra worked. She overthought things way too much and then jumped in all the way, for better or for worse. "In for a penny; in for a pound. What's the worst he can say?"

She picked up the phone and dialed Mark's number, flushing a little at the thought that she'd practically stalked him online, discovering he had no social media presence at all in the process. But her lawyer's research skills were second to none and she'd eventually discovered his number—just for emergencies, she'd told herself at the time.

Rita thinks a year of celibacy counts, Sandra mused.

"Good evening. Stratford Inn. How may I direct your call," a pleasant voice announced.

"Uh," Sandra fumbled, slightly startled. "I think I have the wrong number. I was looking for Mark Cartwright."

"One moment please," came the chirpy response.

Stratford Inn?

The phone rang several times and then the woman was back on the line. "Dr. Cartwright is unavailable at this time. Please call again or leave a message."

Why does he live at a hotel?

"Um...er...This is Sandra Marshall following up about..." *Oh crap. I can't tell this lady my business.* "About my father. I can be reached at any of the numbers on my business card.......Thank you."

Sandra hung up and groaned. "Oh, God! I sounded like I was sixteen. He's going to think I am such an idiot. I don't blame him if he never calls me back!"

She took the bottle into the bathroom and drained a good part of it before she finally emerged from the tub. Just as she was wiping away the suds, the phone rang.

Figuring it was Rita, she wrapped a towel around her hair and put the phone on speaker. "Hey."

"Hello, this is Dr. Mark Cartwright, returning Sandra Marshall's call."

This time Sandra did actually almost drop the phone in the tub. She dove for it and caught it before it hit the suds.

"Hello Dr. Cartwright," Sandra said breathlessly. "Thanks for calling back so soon. I never expected you to interrupt your free time—"

"It's no interruption." His soft voice dragged over her damp skin and Sandra shivered, imagining his hands once again. "I checked on your father today. He's recovering well and should be able to go home by the end of the week. But the nurses very likely told you that when you visited today?"

She turned bright red and grabbed for her robe, talking to her fantasy guy while stark nude a little too hot for comfort. "They did. I guess I just wanted to hear it from you directly. A daughter's worry, you know."

"Certainly."

There was a long, awkward silence, before he spoke again.

"Miss Marshall, I apologize, but my surgical skills are far better than my small talk. Did you—"

At the same time, Sandra had started speaking. "Look, I'm really sorry. The reason I actually called you—"

They stopped at the same time and to her immense relief, he laughed.

"You first, please."

Here goes nothing!

"I was wondering if you would like to go get coffee one day. I mean, if that's not totally violating doctor patient confidentiality. Or something."

"You're not my patient," he replied, and there seemed to be a smile in his voice. "I'd like that. I will warn you though that my, er, dating skills are minimal."

Date? He called it a date!

Grinning from ear to ear, Sandra managed a reply. "Mine are rusty, so I think we'll figure it out. What day works for you?"

"Can we do it sometime after January second? I'm going to visit my parents over Christmas week and I'm booked pretty solidly until then."

She glanced at her calendar. "What about January 6th? Maybe at 8? I work late most days, sorry."

"So do I. That works well. It's a date, Miss Marshall."

"Sandra. Please." Her face ached from the huge smile stretched across it. "I'll see you then, doctor."

"Mark."

"Mark."

"Merry Christmas in advance."

They chatted awkwardly for another moment before hanging up and then Sandra shed her robe and dove straight back into the bath. *I have a date!*

CHAPTER FOUR

He wasn't sure why he felt the need to tell someone, but for some reason, he did. Shortly after Mark returned from his bittersweet Christmas holiday, he walked up to the nurses' station and told Carrie about Sandra. No preliminaries. In typical Mark style, it was just,

"I, uh, have a date."

Carrie spun around from where she'd been pulling a page off the printer. Her eyes bugged out. "You have a what?!" Dropping the printout, she raced around the counter and pulled Mark into a massive hug.

Flustered, Mark stood awkwardly still and patted Carrie's back.

"You have a date!" she crowed, apparently not caring that the entire hallway was now openly staring. "2018 is going to be a great year!"

"For you? Because I have a date?" he said uncertainly, grateful when she finally let go.

"You have no idea how long I've hoped and prayed for this," she informed him, and he was shocked to see a mist in the older woman's usually flinty, pragmatic eyes. "You need someone to love, Mark Cartwright. Badly."

"It's just one date," he protested. "I can't promise any sort of love."

Carrie shook her head, gray curls flying every which way, and propped her hands on her hips. "As long as it's taken you to get to this stage? It's love, honey. And if it's not yet, it will be. Did you tell your parents?"

He frowned. "Carrie, it's one date. I hardly think—"

"Tell them," she said firmly. "Now more than ever, your family needs this kind of news, Mark."

And with that, she walked back to her printout. Oddly, Mark could still see her smiling, even when her head was turned away and he was sure there was nothing on the paper to make her so giddy.

He looked around at the hallway and caught various residents grinning, quickly ducking out of sight when he caught them. Phil winked at him from a doorway, and Owens made some kind of gesture that might have been encouraging or obscene, Mark wasn't sure.

Wrapping up in his heavy coat and scarf, he stepped out into the snow, feeling it even more after his brief Florida sojourn. He hurried to his car, got the heater going, and then pulled out his phone.

He stared at it for a moment before dialing. After a moment, his mother answered.

"Mark? What's wrong?"

"Wrong?"

"We just saw you. You usually don't call for at least a couple weeks after we see you."

"I—" he stopped, atypically guilt-ridden. His father was dying and here he was, going about his life as normal. She was right. He probably wouldn't have called. He just didn't think of things like that, usually.

"Don't, honey," his mom cut into his thoughts. "It's just what you're like. We know you love us, in your own Mark way. What's wrong?" she asked again.

"Nothing," Mark replied, leaning his head back into the seat and staring at the iced-over windows. "I just wanted to tell you something. I thought about it over Christmas, but it was never the right time."

"Now I'm really worried. Mark, what is it?"

"I have a date. Tomorrow, actually, with—"

His words were cut off by his mother's jubilant scream. Then there was laughing and apparently crying too, from what he could tell, and Mark only grew more confused as his father came on the line.

"I'm proud of you, son," Hugh Cartwright rasped, the pain evident in his tone. "You're a good son. Always have been. But it's time you looked beyond the walls of the hospital. This is about the best present you could give me, knowing you're finally putting yourself out there."

By the time he hung up a good while later, the defroster had done its job and Mark could clearly see the wintry scene outside the car's windows. He also finally understood clearly that though he wasn't even 30, his parents' greatest dream was to see him with "a nice girl." Carrie had been right.

SANDRA DIDN'T TELL Rita about the date. She didn't dare, because she knew her best friend would rush right over and try to dress her up to the nines. And it was just a simple pizza dinner, after all. Surely, slacks were fine?

Even so, as she paced back and forth outside the pizza place where she and Mark had agreed to meet, she kept glancing at herself in the window, her reflection fuzzy in the glow of a streetlight, and wondering if maybe she should have at least put on a necklace or blown out her hair. She took pride in her appearance, but after a long day, she'd come home and collapsed for an hour, rather than primping—

"Hi."

She looked up and saw Mark standing a few feet away, that sweet shy smile on his face. "Hi!" Sandra broke into a grin. He had that effect on her, apparently.

"You look lovely." Mark approached her and extended his hand.

Such a gorgeous hand, she mused as she formally shook it.

"That's ... probably not how you usually say hello on a date," he said after a bashful second, letting her fingers go with what Sandra hoped was reluctance.

"It's fine," she reassured him and nodded at the restaurant's door. "Want to go in? I'm freezing."

"I'm sorry. Of course," he pushed the door open and held it for her. "It's just a hole in the wall I come to sometimes."

Sandra walked past him, enjoying the brief moment when she brushed against him before stepping into the small family restaurant.

"This is nice," she said, looking around at the handful of booths, each with a stubby candle in the middle of them. The walls were covered in what looked like family portraits and the small menu was scrawled on a chalkboard.

"Yeah?" Mark smiled and her heart fluttered. "I ... like that you like it. I wasn't sure. My friend Carrie insisted you'd prefer more upscale because of your dad, but that didn't make sense to me. I mean, you're you, and he's him."

Sandra broke into a huge grin. "I like that you get that. I just flat out like you, Mark Cartwright, I think."

Then the teenage waiter, wearing a poorly fitted suit, walked over, took their coats, and guided them to their seats.

"I like the chef's choice pizza," Mark told her, as they settled in. "I never know what I'm getting that way. My daily life is so organized, I like to try at least a little variety on the rare occasion that I'm not working. Don't tell my colleagues, though. They'll need heart surgery."

Sandra laughed, liking him more by the minute. "Chef's choice sounds good. I won't drink, though, if you don't mind. Those roads are too dangerous, even if it's only a glass."

He nodded seriously and a few minutes later their food was ordered, two coffees were on the way, and they were just looking at each other in shy silence.

Finally, Mark spoke. "I'm the world's worst at small talk," he confessed. "But I'd liked to know how your day was. Sincerely."

Impulsively, Sandra reached across the table and placed her hand over his. "My day was awful. But it just got a lot better when you drove up."

He smiled and looked at her hand for a long moment before slowly, carefully, wrapping his fingers around it. "What was so awful?"

She loved having his hand on hers, Sandra immediately discovered. "It was paperwork day. I hate that. I'd rather be in court any day than filing X, Ys, and Zs. But it's something that just has to get done, and I have a bad habit of letting it pile up."

He chuckled, a low, husky sound that hit her in all the right places. "I don't avoid it, but my colleagues probably wish I would. I get it wrong every time. I'm sort of a one-trick pony, I guess. Surgery or nothing."

"My best friend tells me that all the time," Sandra said with a grin. "Get some hobbies, woman," she mimicked Rita's voice. "Get a life!"

"Is it too soon to say maybe we could find some hobbies together?" he asked hesitantly.

"Way too soon," Sandra replied, and squeezed his hand.

"And therefore perfect timing." She watched him work that over in his head before he grinned.

The waiter chose that moment to set their coffees down. They ordered the pizza and then Sandra reached immediately for the small jug of creamer. "How do you take your coffee?"

"I don't know," he admitted. "However I get it, usually. Is it weird that it just doesn't matter to me?"

"Very," she teased, reluctantly letting go of his hand and sitting back, hands cupped around the warmth of the coffee. "How was your own day?"

"If I talk about that, it'll be all I talk about for the rest of the evening," Mark said softly. "I'm sort of obsessive when it comes to my work, people tell me. It was a successful day. Surgery was interesting and patients are doing well. I'd rather talk about you. Is that okay?"

"I'm not that interesting," Sandra said, blushing. "How was your Christmas? You said you were visiting family?"

Mark's smile faded and he looked down at his black coffee, stirring it even though there was nothing added to it. "Sad. My father's not well. That's not great date conversation either, I guess. I'm really bad at this."

"Hey." Sandra nudged his foot under the table until he looked at her, and when he did, the sad confusion in his green eyes broke her heart. "You're doing fine. I'm sorry about your dad, Mark. Tell me about it. I'm guessing you haven't talked to anybody."

"He's dying," Mark said quietly. "And none of my surgical skills can save him."

"Oh," she whispered, "I'm so sorry. I—" Not knowing what else to do or say, Sandra got up and put her arms around the surgeon, drawing him in close. "I don't know if this is okay, but I needed to hug you. I'm sorry, Mark."

After a moment of sitting still, his arms moved around her

and gathered her close. Sandra pressed into his chest, leaning her head on his shoulder. In spite of the reason for the hug, nothing had ever felt quite so right.

Mark scooted over in the booth and automatically, Sandra slid in beside him. She stayed there for the rest of the night as they talked about everything and anything, over bites of some of the best pizza she'd ever had, until the night had flown by and the restaurant was closing.

As they walked to their cars, Mark clumsily reached out and tucked Sandra's scarf closer around her neck. "I had a lot of fun tonight," he told her, his fingers lingering against her cold cheek. "When I tell my sister how well it went, she'll start writing a book about all the ways I shouldn't mess it up."

"Rita will be wedding planning," Sandra said ruefully. "Right after she murders me for not telling her about the date in the first place."

Mark laughed. "Could we do this again?"

"Yes, please." Sandra smiled. "Sooner, rather than later. Doing this again could be a new hobby."

"Or maybe doing this." Slowly, carefully, he took her face in his hands and brushed her lips with his.

It was the sweetest, most innocent kiss and she lit up from inside. "Or maybe this," Sandra agreed, looking into his eyes and forgetting the snow. "This could definitely be a new hobby."

Hesitantly, Mark gathered her closer and she stepped into him eagerly. He tilted his head and gently deepened the kiss. The moment their tongues touched, the gentle heat vanished and they were suddenly devouring, hands roaming, bodies pressed together so intimately it was a wonder there wasn't steam coming off them. Snow fell and the couple kissed and kissed and kissed, lost in one another.

Finally, Sandra stumbled back, staring at him. She touched her kiss-swollen lips. "I love this hobby already."

Mark brushed his thumb over her bottom lip. "I need practice. I want to be as good at that as I am at surgery, Sandra. The best you've ever kissed."

"You already are," Sandra said breathlessly, everything this man said and did touching her in a place far beyond anywhere anyone else had ever reached. "But I am all for practice. Believe me."

Somehow, they managed to avoid getting lost in one another again and she started the drive home. But as she drove, Mark's arms were still around her in her mind, his gentle hands were stroking her face, and he was whispering sweet nothings as he guided her to his bed. She suspected she would get no sleep at all tonight.

CHAPTER FIVE

As Mark walked into the hotel, Melody, the girl at the front desk called out, "Dr. Cartwright I've got phone messages for you. When Mark reached out for the five pink slips, Melody eyed him up and down and asked, "How was your date?"

"What makes you think I was on a date?" asked Mark.

He glanced at the pink sheets. Predictably, the calls were all from Cindy.

"Not exactly rocket science. This is the first time in the three years you've been living here that a woman who isn't a relative has called. And you've got lipstick all over you."

Mark touched his lips and found he wasn't even embarrassed. "You're right. It was a date. And it was amazing." He laughed at her stunned expression and headed upstairs.

"So how did it go?" Cindy asked as soon as she picked up the phone.

"It was great," Mark said simply, stepping into the bathroom before even taking off his coat and grinning at the lipstick.

"Oh my God. Really? Details. I want details!"

"I took her to Marufo's."

"What?" Cindy exclaimed. "Mark, that place is a dump!"

"I took her to Marufo's," he repeated. "I didn't pick her up, because it didn't occur to me. I wore my usual clothes." He kept going even as Cindy sputtered and fumed. "I acted like my normal self, because I don't know how to act like anyone else. And it was amazing."

"How do you know? Mark, what you think is amazing often doesn't line up with anybody else!"

"For one thing, because I have lipstick smeared all over my face. And she wants to see me again. She specifically said she'd like to make it a hobby."

"You kissed?" Cindy shrieked. "Mom will die!"

There was an awkward silence at her choice of words.

"Why is Mom so excited about this?" he finally asked, unwinding his scarf and replaying how Sandra had used it to pull herself in closer.

"Because she really worried that you'd be alone forever, Mark. So did I. So did Dad. It has nothing to do with your age. You just are so neck-deep in the hospital that you barely poke your head out. Mom wants more for you than work. We all do."

"It was just a date," he muttered, even though he knew that it hadn't been. "It doesn't mean anything will necessarily happen in the long term." Even as he spoke, he knew it was a lie. He wanted to get to know Sandra in every possible way. And he could already see a future with her in it.

"Can you imagine coming home to her?" Cindy asked.

Mark looked around at his spartan apartment, at the sterile kitchen table, never used, the couch, rarely used, the walls, devoid of any color or decoration. He imagined Sandra's blue coat draped across the back of a chair, her perfume stored in his empty bathroom cabinet, her shoes thrown across the room after he'd swept her into his arms as she arrived home from work and carried her to bed. He imagined his bed with her lying in it, naked and arms open, reaching for him.

"Yes. I can. I love the sound of her laugh. I like how she listens carefully to what I have to say. I like the way she smells. I like the stories she tells and the dreams she has. I like how intelligent and driven she is. I like how she feels in my arms. And she's the most beautiful woman I've ever seen, to boot. Yes, I can imagine coming home to her or having her come home to me."

"Thank you, Lord," breathed Cindy. "Did you ask her out on a second date?"

"We didn't make official plans," he answered. "But I thought we'd have a tour of the hospital and then dine at the cafeteria."

"Mark Cartwright—"

"You don't get my jokes," he interrupted dryly. "She does. She just gets me. Goodnight, sis." He hung up and stood there in the middle of his empty apartment thinking that over and over again. *She gets me.*

That knowledge felt even better than cutting-edge surgery.

THE NEXT MORNING on his way to breakfast, Mark encountered the hotel's owner, Joanna Newman, yet another of the motherly women who felt the need to keep an eye out for him because they worried about his social ineptitude.

"So, Mark," she said, looking him up and down carefully. "You're looking pretty dapper for hospital rounds. How was your date?"

"It was fine, thank you, Mrs. Newman," Mark replied, stifling the urge to roll his eyes. "How did you know I had a date?"

"We're a small hotel, Mark. Not much goes on here I don't know about."

"So I have discovered," replied Mark.

"So when are you seeing her again?" Joanna inquired.

"Don't you already know?" challenged Mark.

"You smell like fancy cologne and you're wearing hospital clothes, so I'd say after work tonight," Joanna said dryly.

Mark felt his face redden. He hadn't even asked Sandra officially, but yes, he'd hoped for tonight. He needed to see her. To talk to her. To hold her. It had kept him awake half the night to imagine her wrapped in his arms, then sleeping peacefully beside him.

He ducked his head hoping to avoid Joanna Newman's beady stare.

"Mark," she said. "You've been here a long time. Long enough that I consider you family."

"As do I, Mrs. Newman," Mark replied.

"That's why I feel compelled to offer you a piece of advice. You probably think I am a meddlesome old woman." Joanna put up her hand to stop Mark's interruption. "My husband Randall and I worked together to keep this place afloat in the tough years and we built a good life together. My advice is: Take things slow. You can't unring the bell. Make sure before you make a commitment. I know you don't take these things lightly. Make sure this girl doesn't either."

"Thanks, Mrs. Newman. I'll keep that in mind."

"And one other thing, Mark," Mrs. Newman turned to add. "Don't let that sister of yours meddle in your love life. She thinks she knows better and her heart's in the right place. But love is a personal thing. She can't pick for you."

"I'll tell her you said that," Mark teased.

"You do and I'll deny it," retorted Joanna. "And don't let me meddle in your love life either, by the way. You do you, Mark Cartwright. It's what you do best, besides saving lives."

. . .

HE CALLED her on his lunch break, updating her about her dad and also asking her out again. Sandra readily agreed to an immediate second date. When he picked her up—it made sense to him, suddenly, why someone would do that, even if they both had cars—she was dressed casually in brushed denim jeans and jacket and cute ankle boots. The passenger's door of his old Cavalier creaked as he nudged it open.

"I thought it was time you met the other female in my life," he joked, as she slipped into the passenger seat.

"I thought your surgical nurse might be the other woman in your life," Sandra said lightly when he slid in on the other side.

"Honey?" Mark asked, surprised. "What made you think that? Our relationship is strictly professional," he assured her, starting the car and pulling onto the road.

"I'm not sure that's the way she'd like it to be," Sandra said. "With all of Dad's stuff, I had a lot of contact with Honey for about three weeks. The way she talked about you, Mark, the woman's halfway in love. It's fine. I don't have any right to be jealous yet. I just figured you should know."

"You do have a right to be jealous." He reached over and touched her knee lightly. "I wouldn't like it if one of your coworkers was in love with you. But Honey has gone through a nasty divorce and has two kids. She's having difficulty making ends meet and her ex isn't offering child support. Maybe she's into me as kind of a work fantasy. But she doesn't understand me at all. Nobody at works does, really, even though they're really nice about my oddities. Nobody anywhere does, really, except you."

He stopped at a red light, leaned over, and kissed Sandra softly. She tasted as good as the previous night and it was all he could do not to pull her over and drag her into his arms for something much more intense.

"No coworkers are in love with me, I promise," Sandra said

breathlessly, and he smiled, pleased of the effect his kiss had on her.

It was a short drive to La Trattoria, Sandra's restaurant of choice this time. They were greeted warmly by the owner and given a table for two.

"I could get drunk on the aroma alone," Sandra admitted, inhaling deeply.

"That's fresh garlic and mama's special sauce," Mark said smiling. "Nothing is made ahead. Mama rules the kitchen with an iron fist."

Without being asked, the waiter set a basket of garlic bread on the table. This was followed by a small plate on which he drizzled olive oil, a red liquid and a sprinkle of spices.

"Garlic?" Sandra raised an eyebrow. "Maybe I made a mistake suggesting this place."

"If we both taste like it, it'll cancel out the flavor, I think?" Mark said hopefully. "But I don't want any excuse not to kiss you."

"No excuses allowed," she promised, reaching for a piece of bread and groaning as she took a bite. "Okay, yeah. Totally worth garlic breath. Oh my God, this is so good!"

He loved how passionate she was about the smallest things.

As they munched on the warm crusty bread dipped liberally in the olive oil, the two discussed the interrogation they'd been given by Rita and Cindy.

"Rita raked me over the coals for not dressing up," Sandra told him wryly. "How dare I not wear a dress in subzero temperatures."

"I like what you wear," he assured her. "And I almost never notice clothes, so trust me, you've looked beautiful every time I've seen you so far. I can't imagine you ever won't."

"You haven't seen me first thing in the morning," she teased, and he had a vision of her with her hair tousled every which way as she opened her eyes on the pillow beside his.

"I got told off for my restaurant of choice," he told her, in lieu of blurting out how much he wanted to see her the next morning.

"Marufo's? I loved it," Sandra protested. "Heaven help us if they ever meet!" she went on. "It'll be all over except the honeymoon."

"Do you really think my sister would allow me to plan anything as important as a honeymoon?" Mark asked.

"They'd both probably insist on going along," Sandra added.

"And planning all the activities," Mark added.

"Probably rating our performance too," Sandra giggled.

The thought of performing left Mark suddenly aching. He wanted Sandra in every possible way. Leaning across the table, he drew her into a hungry, passionate kiss and relished her low moan. The garlic didn't make one bit of difference, it turned out.

"You make me crazy," he whispered as he drew back, finally. "And I'm not a crazy guy, Sandra. I haven't taken a weekend off in years, but I will this week, if you have time to spend it with me. My family has a cabin not too far away."

"Yes," she said immediately, twining their fingers together. "I never take weekends off either. But absolutely, positively, yes."

CHAPTER SIX

They saw each other every night of the week, including one evening when Sandra initially thought she'd need to cancel because of a late meeting. But Mark was happy with eating at the only restaurant still open, a Waffle House, and he met her there at 11. They talked till 3 in the morning. There was no question in Sandra's mind that she was already falling head over heels for the man and for some reason, that didn't scare her. The pace felt right, just like Mark did.

The two got an early start Saturday morning. Sandra met Mark at the door with a backpack, a cooler, and a small suitcase. He stowed them in the back of his Cavalier and then reached for Sandra, who was already reaching for him.

"Hi," he whispered into her lips. "I get told off a lot for forgetting social niceties like that. I just start talking without saying hello sometimes."

"Hi," she whispered back, gazing up at him starry-eyed. "I like your way of saying hello just fine. But don't you dare try it out on a coworker."

"I love your jealousy," he murmured, cupping her cheek. "But there's no need to be. I'm not interested in anyone else,

Sandra. I honestly never have been. You get that, right? You're my first. In every possible way."

She blinked in total surprise. "I'm your—oh wow."

He flushed. "Yeah. Want to run away screaming before we drive off to an isolated cabin?"

"No," she said firmly. "Not even a little bit. I don't know how other women have been so blind, but I love that I discovered you first. I think I may also want to be your last, Mark. Is that too fast?" It was becoming their thing. Everything was moving so quickly, they often playfully asked each other the question. Only this time, Sandra was dead serious.

"No." He rested his forehead against hers. "It took me almost 30 years to find you. I'm not planning on letting you go anytime soon, believe me."

It was with extreme reluctance that she let him go so that he could drive her to the cabin.

The conversation throughout the hour-long drive was largely about his dreams of working with Doctors Without Borders and her hopes to do far more pro bono work in the near future. They'd both reached the peaks of their respective professions and were ready for new challenges.

As they approached the cabin, the sun was just coming over the White Mountains.

"Oh! It's lovely!" Sandra breathed, staring out at the tall snow-covered pines and rolling hills. "I'm guessing you don't make it out here much?"

"Not in a few years," he admitted, turning the car onto a dirt road. "Cindy and I used to spend summers here with our grandparents. We'd come back to school brown as berries from all the swimming and hiking and be wild children for two weeks afterwards, while we settled down. I don't know how our teachers stood us."

"I love the idea of Mark the wild child," Sandra said with a smile. "My family was way big city. We didn't do much outdoors. So this is my first. Be gentle with me."

He grinned. "That's a promise. And I promise we'll come out here often, if you like it."

He parked the car in front of a small cabin right beside a frozen-over creek. "I hired someone to clean the place out and get it ready for us," he told her as they grabbed their bags. "He promised to have a cord of wood stacked too."

A moment later, they were inside and indeed, Mark's hired hand had given the cabin a good going over, dusting, removing the covers from the furniture, and generally sprucing the place up so it didn't look at all as though it had been empty for years.

Sandra looked around at the small kitchenette, the coffee table, and the battered, low-slung couch in front of the fireplace, filled with the promised kindling. Her eyes drifted to the rug, imagining wrapping around Mark and teaching him a thing or two as the firelight moved over their bare skin.

He encircled her waist from behind and whispered in her ear, "I can hear your thoughts. I want that too, Sandra. But if we start now, we'll never leave the cabin. That much, I can promise you."

"I do actually want to do a little hiking," she admitted, turning in his arms to kiss him warmly. "Can we see the lake, even if swimming is out of the question for another five months, at least?"

"Sure. We can picnic there," he suggested, nodding at the cooler she'd packed. "It'll be cold, but it takes about an hour to hike there anyway, so we'll have warmed up some. You said you had sandwiches?"

Lunches stowed away in their backpacks, they headed out into the forest with Mark leading the way. Sandra peppered him with questions about the various trees and landscape features, knowing next to nothing about the great outdoors. He told her what he could about the difference between spruces and firs and birch trees, and each time they stopped to examine an interesting plant or rock, they also took the time to warm up with a hungry kiss.

Her nose ran from the cold and her ears tingled beneath her beanie. Rita would die at what a mess she looked, probably, but Sandra didn't care. She inhaled the rich forest smell and realized with a start that it was a lot like how Mark smelled all the time. It was like he carried some of this place with him all the time. She liked that idea a lot.

Stopping at a little outcropping to adjust her shoelace, she called out to tell him she'd halted and found her foot slipping on a patch of unexpected scree. "Mark," she began, flailing, and he turned toward her, alarm evident on his face. "Mark!" Sandra yelped, losing her balance completely and toppling sideways.

The surgeon lunged for her, but she was already careening off the edge of the low outcropping, shouting in pain as she hit the ground on her side and rolled a good ways down the short slope.

SEEING SANDRA FALL, even when there was absolutely no mortal danger from such a short height, left Mark dry mouthed. He dropped his backpack and

scrambled down after her, yelling. "Sandra? Sandra! Say something!"

"I'm okay," she whispered, as he arrived at her side and dropped to his knees where she lay crumpled. "Just my leg. Hurts."

He was far more concerned about her head, which had a sizable swelling already starting at her temple. Mark smoothed her hair back and kissed her pale cheek, brushing away the dirt and gravel embedded in it. Seeing her wide eyes staring up at him brought an up-welling of relief that should have been illogical because, again, the danger was minimal. Nevertheless, seeing her alert and alive left him almost weak kneed with relief.

"Lie still, sweetheart," he ordered, automatically using the endearment when even 'honey' was completely foreign to him. "I have a first aid kit in my bag."

"I'm okay," she said again, trying to sit up and gasping with pain.

"Don't," Mark warned, easing her back down. "Let me check you out first."

"I love it whenever you check me out," she joked weakly.

He smiled faintly and did a quick visual assessment before palpating her limbs and torso. "Not how I'd wanted to run my hands over you for the first time," he teased her, kissing Sandra softly. "I'm worried about a concussion and a possible hairline fracture for that ankle you fell on. We should get you to the ER for an X-ray."

Sandra went so pale that Mark frowned in dismay. "What?" he asked worriedly. "Does it hurt really badly suddenly?"

"No ... I ... just ... no hospitals. Please, Mark." A tear slipped down her cheek. "I hate them."

"But I work at a hospital," he said in confusion, then realized this was the wrong time. He kissed the tear away. "Let's get you back to the cabin, first. Then I can do a more thorough assessment."

"Do my pants have to come off for that?" she joked, catching his hand and kissing it. "I'm sorry, Mark. I ruined everything."

"Shhh. Nothing's ruined at all. It'll hurt when I mess with that ankle, though. I'm sorry," he apologized in advance, scrambling up the slope and retrieving his bag. Breaking open the first aid kid, he pulled out a bandage. Sandra visibly gritted her teeth as he wrapped her ankle, but didn't otherwise complain.

"I'm so lucky I was hiking with you," she muttered through clenched teeth. "For more reasons than just this."

He smiled and finished fixing the wrap in place. "I used to hike with a very clumsy sister. You don't know how many times my bandages and splints came in handy. Now let's get you back to the trail. You're going to need to lean on me heavily. Carrying you would be romantic, but also suicidal. I prefer my romance without a side of bloodshed."

"I love your sense of humor," she sighed.

It was a struggle, but with her holding tightly to Mark, they fought their way up the short incline. He located a branch that was the right height for a crutch and with Sandra leaning on his shoulder, they hobbled back to the cottage, resting frequently.

Once they were clear of the trees and on totally flat ground, Mark scooped Sandra into his arms. "Now romance is safe," he teased, hurrying toward the cabin in the distance. "I love having you in my arms, by the way."

She burrowed into him in a way that turned his heart over. "I love being in them."

When they got back to the cabin, Mark settled her on the couch, elevated her leg, and packed ice into a towel, then applied the improvised ice pack to her ankle. He didn't see any signs of a concussion and there was swelling and bruising, but the ankle ultimately appeared to be badly sprained, not broken.

"So no broken bones?" Sandra asked. "That means no hospital, right?"

"You need to get it x-rayed when we get back to Portsmouth," he replied, tucking a cover around her and kneeling in front of the fire to get it going.

"But if it's better by the time we leave, then maybe x-rays won't be necessary?" Sandra asked hopefully.

"I don't know about that," Mark answered, coaxing the flames to life. "You hadn't told me you don't like hospitals."

She didn't answer, and he didn't press her, in spite of his curiosity. Once the fire was roaring steadily, he turned back to Sandra and found her watching him with sad eyes.

"What?" he asked with concern, going over to her. "Tell me."

"I really did mess everything up. I brought stuff to rustle up a great dinner in the kitchen. And sexy underwear."

He grinned and hugged her carefully to him. "How about you call instructions to me in the kitchen?" he suggested, kissing her bruised temple very gently. "And you can describe the underwear to me, so I can anticipate it next time."

"How about you sit here and kiss me for a while until the fire warms us up?" she countered. "And then dinner and description."

In response, Mark tossed pillows every which way and shifted Sandra so she sat on his lap sideways, her leg still extended and elevated on the coffee table. "Your wish is this doctor's command," he murmured, drawing her into a slow-simmering kiss that didn't end for a very long time.

CHAPTER SEVEN

At some point, Mark carried her to the bedroom, and like the gentleman he was, slept on the couch. Sandra herself slept fitfully. Her ankle ached, and her dreams were hot and sweaty filled with images of the handsome doctor only a few steps across the hall.

As the morning sun began to seep beneath the curtains, she heard a knock on the door and sat up slightly, wincing. "Come in!"

Mark pushed the door open and the irresistible fragrance of coffee immediately filled the room. He was unshaven and tousle-headed and looked so good that Sandra wished she could walk across the room and kiss him hard.

"How are you feeling?" Mark asked, walking over and placing the coffee on the nightstand.

"Like I wish you'd spent the night with me," she groused.

"One day very soon," he said with a smile, and kissed her long and slow before moving to examine her ankle. "It looks a lot better this morning," Mark noted approvingly.

"So no break?" Sandra asked.

"It's still too swollen to tell." He sat down on the bed beside her. "You're even prettier first thing in the morning than I imagined."

She blushed. "I have morning breath. My hair probably still has pine needles in it. I've got dirt still on my fa—"

He cut her off with a hungry kiss. "I've never seen a woman first thing in the morning before, besides my mother and sister. And even if I had, you're still more beautiful than anyone else would be. I'm a surgeon. I know human bodies. Trust me."

She could've swooned at his bumbling, earnest compliments. "Mark, is it too soon to say I'm falling?" she blurted out before she could stop herself.

He looked into her eyes, his own dark and intense suddenly. "No. I am too, but this fall carries less risk of broken bones, I think. Unless I mess it up. I really don't know what I'm doing, Sandra. I wanted to bring you breakfast in bed, but I can't cook any better than you can probably do a surgical stitch. I wanted to bring you flowers—women like those, right?—but they're all frozen. So, uh, all I could do was this."

Curiously, Sandra unfolded the paper he abruptly thrust at her and when she saw the carefully sketched drawing of a rasher of bacon, eggs, and a steaming cup of coffee on a wooden table, with a single rose bud in a vase, her eyes welled up.

"What?" Mark said in alarm. "People usually like my drawings. I developed the talent when I was illustrating a surgical textbook. I like precision and—"

Sandra stopped him with a hard hug, pressing her face into his broad chest. "I love your drawings. And dammit, Mark. I'm close to loving you. How is that possible after just a week of dates?"

He rested his chin in her hair and stroked her back a little awkwardly, making her smile at his innocence. "I figure you and I are making our own rules. We're not like other people. Why should we follow the things they dictate for love and friendship?"

"Falling so hard," Sandra sighed, drawing back and scooting over on the bed. She masked her wince so he wouldn't fuss over her ankle. "Come curl up with me. Please? I'll behave ..."

He blushed. "Sandra, I would. Except I don't have any self-control left, honestly. You look so soft and warm. And you mentioned that underwear. I'll embarrass myself. When I woke up this morning, it was all I could do not to wake you up with kiss after kiss."

It was the sweetest thing to see her virgin boyfriend fumbling his way through an apology about how he'd woken up hard and would very likely explode if he so much as slid his hand beneath her shirt right now. Sandra masked a smile and took pity on him.

"Okay, handsome. Then at least carry me to the kitchen so I can order you around. I need sustenance and I bet I can talk you through making an egg or three. I brought some of those in the cooler. I'd sort of been hoping to be the one to make us breakfast for our morning after."

Mark scooped her up, blankets and all, and carried her into the living room. He settled her on the couch, then dragged it right up to the kitchen, ensuring her foot was securely elevated before picking up a frying pan and waving it like a sword.

"Avast, fair maiden. Your knight in shining scrubs awaits your directives."

She laughed. "So cheesy, it should be on a pizza. Okay. Here's how egg surgery is performed, generally speaking ..."

CHAPTER EIGHT

There was no lovemaking that weekend, but there was plenty of kissing, once Mark came down off his morning high, and there was also no hospital, thankfully, when Sandra's ankle swelling lessened considerably by Sunday afternoon when they drove back home.

In spite of the change in plans, she had more fun playing board games with Mark, arguing over whether his surgical terms were actually Scrabble-valid or not, than she could ever remember having on any other date. Her seven months with Adam couldn't hold a candle to a week with virgin Mark Cartwright, Sandra reflected after he dropped her off and promised to call her the next day.

She soaked happily in the tub and waited expectantly for the call which came around 8 pm.

"Hi Rita," Sandra said without looking at the Caller ID.

"Did you just get in?" Rita asked.

"No. I've been here since early afternoon."

There was dead silence on the other end of the line. "What happened?" Rita asked. "How did you screw this up?"

"Well thanks for that vote of confidence. What makes you think I screwed up?"

"Well, you're home early," Rita pointed out. "Is that Mark's fault?"

"No. It's mine," Sandra admitted.

"I knew it!" Rita said triumphantly. "What did you do?"

"I kinda rolled down a hill and sprained my ankle."

"Is it broken?" Rita asked in concern.

"No it's just a bad sprain. Mark put a splint on it. He bandaged it and made me a crutch. Then when we got back to the cabin he elevated it and put ice on it. But it precluded any outdoor activities."

"I'll bet it precluded bedroom gymnastics too," Rita guessed.

"Don't be so crude, Rita. What makes you think there would have been bedroom activities anyhow?" Sandra demanded, totally hypocritically. It just bugged her that Rita would assume, even if she also had.

"Oh, please! A couple goes to a remote cabin for the weekend? What do you suppose would go on? Roasting marshmallows?"

"We did actually roast marshmallows. His fingers got all sticky when he tried to pull it off the stick and then he fed it to me and we laughed like crazy when the goo got stuck in both our hair somehow, after he kissed me."

"Ultra-romantic," Rita teased.

"Mark wanted me to go and have x-rays," Sandra confessed. "For my ankle."

"Did you tell him about your hospital phobia?"

"I told him it was a story for later," mumbled Sandra.

"Later isn't going to make it easier," Rita cautioned. "Sooner or later he's going to have to know. The guy's a surgeon. It's a slight stumbling block to true love, Sandra."

"I know that. It's just so ridiculous. I'm ashamed."

"Well, get over it. You said he gets all of you. That long-time phobia is definitely a part."

"Yes, Mother." Sandra rolled her eyes.

That night, Sandra's sleep was crowded with images of Mark's lean, hard, toned body. She moaned as she imagined his hot kisses. His lips were all over her. His hands caressed, kneaded, and flitted to her most intimate spots, learning her for the very first time. For his very first time.

She could hear his voice whispering sweet words and feel his hot breath on her ear.

Sandra woke with a burning desire in her core. Her ears were buzzing and her mouth felt as dry as an autumn leaf.

MARK GOT EVEN LESS sleep than Sandra. Even a three-mile run and a cold shower didn't banish his fantasies of Sandra in her black underwear, wrapped all around him, every which way.

I can't stand much more of this, Mark thought, toweling off his hair. *How many cold showers can one body sustain?*

As he reached for his pants, finding them overly tight as they usually were these days, in spite of the shower, his phone rang. "Hello," he barked into the receiver.

"Well aren't we cheerful?" his sister commented. "So, little brother, I take it you didn't get laid?"

"You know, I'm not *that* bad a catch!" Mark snapped. "I may be socially clueless, but some people actually like me. Supposedly Honey's halfway in love with me."

"Easy, little bro. Did the luscious lawyer lady turn you down?"

"No the luscious lawyer lady tumbled down the hill like Jack and Jill, thereby putting a huge crimp in the week-end activities."

"Mark, I'm so sorry," said Cindy, and her contrite tone mollified Mark. "Is she okay?"

"Other than a sprained ankle, she's fine," responded Mark. "I wrapped it, iced it, elevated it and deposited her in her condo threatening her with x-rays if she didn't stay off it. Seems the lady has a hospital phobia."

"And dating a doctor? That is too ironic for words," Cindy chuckled.

"I fail to see the humor," Mark commented dryly.

"So when are you seeing her again?"

"Next week-end. Same time. Same location. Except I'll be walking behind her this time, to make sure there are no more tumbles."

"Well, that's a good sign. Seems the lawyer lady is capable of bouncing back."

"Sandra's tough," he informed her. "All the way up the slope and hobbling along on a makeshift crutch she never whimpered or complained—unlike another female who tumbled down that same slope."

"I was in excruciating pain," Cindy defended. "And you weren't very gentle either. Never mind, little brother. You'll get lucky next week-end."

"I sure hope so, sis," sighed Mark. "I'm getting awfully sick of cold showers and long runs."

"Having hot dreams, Mark?" asked his sister.

"You're enjoying this. Aren't you?" he accused.

"Mark, I am just so relieved to discover you have urges. I was about ready to give up on you. Welcome to the human race."

"Funny, Cindy," Mark said before he hung up to the sound of her laughter.

CHAPTER NINE

Mark and Sandra talked briefly every day that week but their busy schedules didn't allow time for any dates this time around. Mark went through definite withdrawal, missing her smell, her smile, her laugh, the feel of her pressed close against him.

Sandra assured Mark her ankle was better. She sent him pictures to show how much the swelling had gone down. Seeing her healing ankle was great, but the slice of her leg that the photos also displayed only added to Mark's nightly fantasies. He longed to kiss that long, smooth curve. Maybe even to lightly draw his teeth along it, if that was something people actually did.

I'm as randy as a teenager! Mark thought, now obsessively worrying about a disastrous first time because he was so damn hungry for this woman, when he'd barely noticed another one before.

When Friday finally arrived, Mark had never been so relieved as when he pulled up in front of Sandra's place, jumped out, pulled her into his arms, and felt in her kiss that she'd missed him just as much.

"I wondered if I'd imagined how good this is," he whispered into her lips. "How good we are."

"You didn't imagine it," she whispered back, kissing him so hungrily he finally had to back away.

"We have to stop. Otherwise, I'm either going to chase you inside to your bedroom or invite you to join me in the back seat."

"I've been fantasizing about that rug in front of the fire," she admitted. "Hold out just a little longer?"

"I can see your dreams and mine have been talking to one another," Mark murmured, dragging a hand down his face nevertheless.

On the drive down, they caught up with each other's respective worlds. It was always so easy to talk to Sandra. And when they weren't talking, Mark enjoyed the silences between them that were now totally comfortable.

"What did your sister say about my doofus tumble down the bank?" asked Sandra.

"She wanted to make sure you were okay and she said to tell you she fell down that same slope when she was twelve."

"Somehow that doesn't make me feel better."

"She also asked why I was in such a bad mood and then proceeded to tell me my attitude would be a lot sunnier if I had gotten laid."

"She said that?" Sandra exclaimed.

"Yes and she added she was relieved to discover I had joined the human race."

"That must have made you feel warm all over. I hate that people seem to think you're a robot," she muttered.

"It doesn't bother me," he promised. "Their problem, not mine. But my vote is that we keep you away from any hiking trails until I've explored you..." his eyes darted toward hers, "thoroughly. With surgical thoroughness."

"That definitely shouldn't sound so sexy," she groaned.

The rest of the drive was laden with sexual tension that wouldn't go away, no matter what they discussed.

AT THE CABIN, Sandra unpacked the groceries while Mark lit the fire, staying far away from each other by unspoken mutual agreement until all the elements of the weekend were in order.

Just one thing to do first, she told herself firmly, as she opened a bottle of wine, grabbed two glasses, and headed back to the living room.

She dropped down beside Mark on the couch and handed him a glass. "It's cozy here," she said burrowing her bare feet into the rug.

"Okay," she said, taking a big gulp of her wine. "I think it's time I told you my hospital story. You'll probably think I'm irrational."

"Most of our fears are irrational," Mark pointed out. "That doesn't make them any less scary."

"You're sweet to say that," she said planting a quick kiss on his cheek. "When I was ten my best friend, Mia, and I were inseparable. We went to school together, played the same sports, and hung out on week-ends. It was rare to see us not together. We called ourselves the Hardy Girls. Then Mia got sick. Everyone kept telling me she was getting better. She was in and out of hospital. Each time I went to see her, she looked smaller and grayer."

She could see from the expression on Mark's face that this was hitting home on a very personal level. It was likely his father was going to go down the same road before long. But Sandra had no choice but to finish the story. She grabbed his hand and pressed it hard as she went on.

"She lost all her beautiful blonde hair. She could no longer do cartwheels, and swim and run. I used to go and visit her in the hospital and read to her and feed her ice chips. Mia seemed to shrink every time I saw her. We once joked that soon the only thing left would be her voice. Then one day when I got to the hospital to surprise her with a new book, Mia's room was empty. She was just...gone. She didn't even leave her voice."

A tear trickled down Sandra's cheek. Mark wiped it away with his thumb. "I'm sorry, sweetheart. I see things from the surgeon's side. Sometimes I forget what things look like from a loved one's perspective."

"I blamed the doctors for not fixing what was wrong with her." Sandra pressed his hand to her cheek, drawing strength from his warm touch. "I blamed the nurses for making her disappear. I blamed myself for not trying hard enough to keep Mia from disappearing. I was a heartbroken, confused, angry ten-year-old. I had nightmares, that because I spent so much time in Mia's room, the evil forces that made her disappear would come and get me next."

"Understandable," said Mark, handing her a tissue. "You were ten."

"And until my father's surgery, I never again darkened the door of a hospital," Sandra admitted, blowing her nose and drying her eyes. "Honestly, being anywhere near them makes me queasy."

To her vast relief, instead of making fun of her or being upset, Mark hugged her close. "A lot of people don't like hospitals, probably for similar reasons. You're not abnormal, Sandra. It's okay. Let me ask you this: What if I feared courtrooms or jails or judges or even lawyers? Would that change your view of me?"

"Of course not!" Sandra exclaimed. "Why would you even have to ask?"

"My point exactly," replied Mark. "It's not like we're ever going to make out in a hospital supply closet... Although I do have some fantasies that involve hospital beds," he said with a grin.

"And I have some fantasies that involve this fluffy rug and a roaring fire." The realization that her fear really wasn't any big deal at all when it came to their relationship left Sandra almost breathless with relief.

Mark leaned over and kissed her. It was a long searching kiss full of passion and promise. "Let's act on those fantasies, shall we?" he murmured in her ear, and she wrapped her arms around his neck and let him carry her the short distance to the rug. He lowered her carefully and followed immediately, his body hard and hungry as it pressed over hers.

Slowly, they peeled the clothes from each other and she saw the awe in Mark's eyes as he looked at her for the first time, and knew her own amazement must be reflected in her own. It was a different first for her as she taught him what she knew and watched the straight A student rise to the challenge in more ways than one, following up on every place she wanted kissed with a suggestion of his own that he somehow knew would be even more erotic.

The man undid her completely and when he finally came into her, his eyes wide with wonder, Sandra lifted to kiss him hard, guiding him through the rise and fall of their hips as one.

Predictably, it didn't last long, but that made no difference to how sweet it was as Mark cried out and came, with Sandra following close behind him. They rested afterwards, holding each other close, the firelight dancing over them as she'd dreamed.

"I love you," Mark said quietly, smoothing the hair back from Sandra's face. "I know it's too fast, but I don't care. That was more than I could ever have dreamed and I dreamed a lot, Sandra. You're more than I could ever have dreamed."

She rolled onto her back and drew him halfway on top of

her, running her hands over the hard planes of his broad chest. "I love you too," she murmured. "It's way too fast, and I don't care either. You're it for me, Mark."

His kiss was as tender as the previous ones had been hot and hungry. They lay by the fire talking and sipping wine until they were both ready to go again and this time Mark carried her to the bed, where Sandra continued to learn the benefits of a loving a man who stopped at nothing to achieve perfection, including following explicit instructions and then experimenting with his own strategies to ensure she came over and over again.

CHAPTER TEN

Mark woke in the early hours of the morning and found Sandra already awake beside him, her eyes locked on him.

"Hey," he said with a smile, reaching out to draw her close to his bare body. "Sleep stalking me?"

She answered with a long kiss. "I loved watching you sleep. I woke up about 45 minutes ago for some reason and just lay here watching you, thinking how lucky I am that I could kiss you awake if I wanted."

"Why didn't you?" he asked curiously.

"I don't know. It was just peaceful thinking about waking up before you forever and always knowing you'll be there." Her eyes met his. "Too fast?"

"Not even slightly," he promised, smoothing his hand down her side before bending his head to kiss one of her beautiful breasts, suckling on the tip and loving the needy moans that Sandra immediately made. "God, I love you. Love you. Love you."

He lifted her on top of him and was about to ask her to show him how this position worked when the phone rang. Mark groaned and let his head drop back against the pillow. Almost at the same time, Sandra's phone shrilled.

"Cindy."

"Rita."

They spoke at the same time.

"If we don't answer, they'll send the cops," Mark sighed, kissing Sandra regretfully. "Rain check?"

"Mmm," she murmured. "Just as long as you cash it in immediately after we talk them down."

"Deal."

The phones rang and rang and the pair went their separate ways to retrieve the devices.

"I was busy," Mark informed his sister as he answered.

"Mark." Cindy's voice was choked with tears and he immediately went rigid. "Mark, it just—I—Dad—Mark, he's gone."

THE FUNERAL WAS MORE of a celebration of Hugh Cartwright than a time for mourning, the many people whose lives the veterinarian had touched taking turns to tell stories about him alongside videos of his shy, playful side, so reflected in his son, clips of his favorite movies, and a backdrop of his favorite songs.

Even so, Sandra watched Hugh's son, the man she'd fallen head over heels in love with, stand beside her pale and silent, his face taut with grief that he didn't quite know how to express.

She didn't try empty platitudes, already knowing Mark wouldn't appreciate them. Not knowing what to do beside holding onto his hand and not letting go for anything, she just sat next to him and hoped that somehow her presence gave him some kind of comfort.

Once the service was concluded and the graveyard had mostly emptied, did Mark attempt any kind of speech as he stared down at the freshly turned earth beneath which his father lay.

"I miss him already. Too fast?"

"No, baby," Sandra replied, wrapping her arm around his waist. "Not even slightly."

"I should be glad he died in his sleep and didn't suffer an agonizing end. I've seen so many of those on the job. But I'm not. I didn't get to say goodbye. I don't even know what I would have said. I suck at words. All I know how to do, really, is cut people open, Sandra."

"You know plenty more," she said firmly. "Your dad was proud of you, Mark. You told me how excited he and your mother were that you'd finally found someone. I know you'll think it's unscientific, but I think maybe he was just holding on until he knew you'd be okay."

He said nothing, continuing to stare at the ground, his eyes empty and broken.

"Mark."

The couple both jumped a little at the unexpected voice and turned to find Chrissy Cartwright standing a few feet away, her own face a mask of deepest grief. Even so, her voice was steady as she spoke again.

"I've barely had a chance to meet your lovely lady. Please don't rush back home. Give me a little time, son. Your father showed us how little time we all have."

Mark nodded once. "I'll stay, Mom. Sandra will need to get back to work, but I'm not going anywhere for at least a few days."

"I'll stay," Sandra said hesitantly, not sure if she was intruding. "If you want me to, I mean. I finally found something way more important than a courtroom victory."

"Yes. Stay." Again, he nodded, holding her hand even tighter. "Please."

Chrissy smiled a little bit and wiped her damp eyes. "48 years and I'll still count our anniversaries even now that he's gone. When you find the right person to walk through life with, it's forever, son. There's no goodbye. Not in your heart or your soul. I know he's just around the corner waiting for me to one day join him. Your father died so happy. Thank you." Not typically an emotional woman, she nevertheless walked over and kissed her son's cheek, pressed his shoulder, then turned to Sandra. "Welcome to the family."

EPILOGUE

"Ma!" Baby Hugh crowed victoriously as he singsonged the word he'd only recently discovered. "Mamamamamama!"

"That's your mama," Mark agreed, kissing his son's blond head, so like Sandra's. "She's on TV because she's helping people, son. She's speaking out for those who don't have voices, representing those who would otherwise have no chance at justice in the courtroom."

"Mamamamamamamama," Hugh babbled happily, oblivious to his father's words.

"I'm so proud of her," Mark went on, talking to his son like he always did. It wasn't baby talk, but he didn't know how to go about that, and both Hugh and his wife seemed to be fine with that.

A year and a half into marriage, things had only gotten better for the couple. Hugh Sr.'s sudden death had changed everything in the sense that it had woken the two workaholics up to how short life really was. A few months after the funeral, Mark had proposed with his grandmother's ring. A few more months and they'd been married in a simple ceremony that neither Cindy nor Rita were necessarily happy about, since it lacked almost any frills or traditional 'romantic' details, but their wedding in Marufo's summer garden, with Cindy wearing a delicate white sheath and wildflowers in her hair, had been beyond any of Mark's dreams. Given that he'd never dreamed of a wedding at all, that wasn't exaggerating. And then when she'd told him she was pregnant...

Mark smiled, reliving that day and the months that followed as his beautiful wife grew big with their child. When she developed preeclampsia and had to be hospitalized, he'd taken a leave of absence from work and sat by her side through it all, helping her through her phobia even as he also cared for her from a medical perspective.

Ultimately, the two of them had moved on to different jobs that didn't require such single-minded focus, Sandra doing the pro bono work she'd always dreamed of, and Mark alternating between Doctors Without Borders stints and work at a local community hospital. The two of them were partners in every way, so when he needed to leave for a few days or even a couple of weeks, Sandra stepped up to the plate and reduced her working hours to be with their son. And Mark did the same for her.

All in all, he was living a dream he never wanted to wake from.

"Hi handsome."

Mark looked over his shoulder in surprise as Sandra walked through the door to their home, the home they'd designed together and which he now looked forward to coming home to far more than a hotel.

"Hi!" He rose to greet her but she was already halfway to him, kicking off her shoes and sliding onto the couch beside him and Hugh, who babbled in delight and clambered straight from

Mark's arms into Sandra's. She kissed his pudgy cheeks and then turned to kiss Mark.

"I thought you wouldn't be home until late," he said, lifting his wife and son both onto his lap and pretending to groan under their combined slight weight.

"I missed you guys," she said simply, resting her head against his shoulder and wrinkling her nose at the sight of herself on TV. "Do you have to watch my every interview?"

"Yes," Mark replied. "I'm proud of my wife. Have I told you that recently?"

"Every time I turn my head," she said with a smile, tilting her head up to look at him even as she bounced Hugh to entertain him. "I roped Rita into babysitting for us tonight. I want you all to myself for a few hours and Hugh loves her so much I figure it's a win for all three of us."

"I'm here," Rita called from the doorway, and Hugh erupted into delighted cheers, waving his arms and almost wriggling off his mother's lap.

A few minutes later the pair were on their way to their favorite restaurant, but before they turned onto the street, Mark pulled over into a parking lot and Sandra, already anticipating the move, was already unbuckling her seat belt. She moved over into his arms and he held her tight, tangling his fingers in her beautiful hair, knowing she wouldn't complain that he'd messed it up.

"I love you," he whispered into her lips, pushing the seat back so they had more room. "Dinner can wait a few minutes. Right now all I want is you, Sandra Cartwright."

"You have me, Dr. Cartwright," she whispered back, blue eyes smiling into his. "You had me at hello."

"You know, I don't think I actually said hello," he realized abruptly. "Sometimes I skip that ..."

Laughing, Sandra cut him off with a kiss. "It's from a song.

But you can say hello now, as many times as you think are necessary to make up for that long ago lapse."

"Hello," Mark murmured between kisses. "Hello. Hello."

The best part of it all, as they held each other close and made out like teenagers, was that they both knew that there would never be a goodbye.

THE END.

ABOUT THE AUTHOR

Mrs. Love writes about smart, sexy women and the hot alpha billionaires who love them. She has found her own happily ever after with her dream husband and adorable 6 and 2 year old kids.

Currently, Michelle is hard at work on the next book in the series, and trying to stay off the Internet.

"Thank you for supporting an indie author. Anything you can do, whether it be writing a review, or even simply telling a fellow reader that you enjoyed this. Thanks

❀ Created with Vellum

CPSIA information can be obtained
at www.ICGtesting.com
Printed in the USA
BVHW071043130223
658402BV00018B/696

9 781648 080036